DEAR BABY

By Courtney Westwood

Illustrations by Louise Rabey

To my own dear babies, my adored husband,

and my supportive family.

-Courtney

To my Auntie Marilyn and Auntie Nancy

who would have loved to have seen this project brought to life,

and to the rest of my family for their continued support.

-Louise

Dear Baby,

We awoke one day and life was the same,
and then in one moment everything changed.

Until that moment we didn't know yet,
how much we could love one we haven't met.

Now that we know that you're on your way,

we'll think of you as we count down the days.

What will you look like? We haven't a clue.

Will your hair have curls? Will your eyes be blue?

We promise to love you and share what we know,

we'll cheer you on as you learn and grow.

One day we'll send you off to start school,
a place we hope you'll find exciting and cool.

From some you will learn and others you'll teach,
with perseverance everything is in reach.

You might not succeed when you try a new thing,

but making mistakes is part of learning.

Meeting new friends might seem a bit scary,
but it isn't hard when you're kind and caring.

Be confident in yourself in all that you do,

we know that you'll thrive if you be the best you!

Someday you'll set off to make it on your own,
but remember that you are never alone.

Whatever you need, we're never too far,

we'll be here for you, wherever you are.

Go into the world and make your impact,
let your passions guide you to stay on track.

Your actions will be your key to success,
with lots of hard work you are sure to impress.

Whatever you choose, we'll be proud of you,
find your happiness and to yourself stay true.

In the future you might pledge yourself to another,
it will be a day unlike any other.

Life will have its ups and also its downs,
support each other through the smiles and frowns.

Work as a team, see through one another's eyes,
when you don't agree, find a compromise.

Make time for each other to have some fun,

create memories you'll treasure for years to come.

Say "I love you" each and every day,

and let your love show in all you do and say.

Caring for one so small can seem a huge task,
but trust your instincts and when you need help, ask.

Promise to love them and share what you know,
be there to cheer them on as they learn and grow.

You'll make us so proud in all that you do,

and we'll love your baby just as we love you.

Most of all we wish you a contented life,
with happiness and joy outweighing strife.

For now, we will wait with nothing but joy,
until we can meet our little girl or boy.

Forever and ever,
Your loving parents.

Printed in Poland
by Amazon Fulfillment
Poland Sp. z o.o., Wrocław

53198732R00021